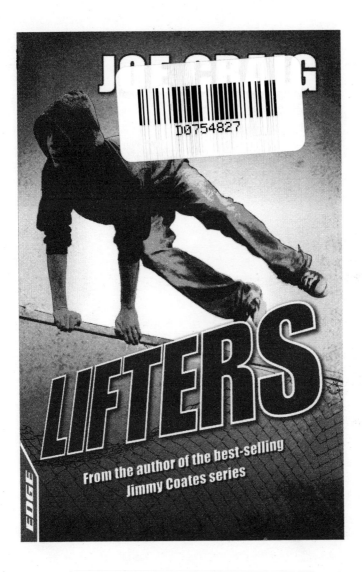

JOE CRAIG

LIFTERS

From the author of the best-selling
Jimmy Coates series

EDGE

Also by Joe Craig:

The *Jimmy Coates* series

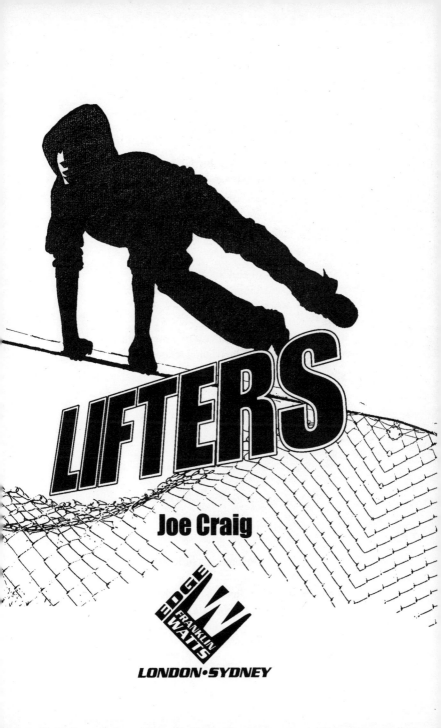

LIFTERS

Joe Craig

EDGE FRANKLIN WATTS

LONDON·SYDNEY

Part of the **RÏVETS** series

First published in 2011
by Franklin Watts

Text © Joe Craig 2011
Cover design by Peter Scoulding

Franklin Watts
338 Euston Road
London NW1 3BH

Franklin Watts Australia
Level 17/207 Kent Street
Sydney, NSW 2000

A CIP catalogue record for this book
is available from the British Library.

Cover credit: Ju-Lee/istockphoto

ISBN: 978 1 4451 0555 0

1   3   5   7   9   10   8   6   4   2

Printed in Great Britain

Franklin Watts is a division of Hachette Children's Books,
an Hachette UK company.
www.hachette.co.uk

To Sarah Manson, Adrian Cole, Joe Keogh, Andy Briggs, Kristy Bishop, Coralie Sleap and all the staff at Drink, Shop & Do, where I wrote this: thank you. And to Mary-Ann Craig: all the inexpressible you already know.

Chapter One

"Go! Go!" Adaq threw himself into the passenger seat. His sister, Maya, hadn't even stopped the car completely, just slowed down enough for him to jump in. She veered back out into the traffic while Adaq was still hauling the door shut.

"You get it?" she asked.

Adaq didn't respond. Of course he'd got it.

"Anyone see you?"

Adaq forced out a laugh. He managed to sound calm while he wiped his hand across his face to hide the shaking.

"How much?" Maya asked. She was always so focused on the money. "How much?" She had one hand on the wheel, the other held out to Adaq.

"Wait," said Adaq. "Give me a chance and I'll—"

As he opened the wallet his mouth stopped working: he'd never seen so much cash. Maya glanced across and for a second she went as quiet as her brother. The growl of the traffic around them sounded like the city cheering their triumph.

"Oh-my-god," Maya gasped. She jerked the wheel, cutting across two lanes, and slammed on the brakes to pull up under a railway bridge. Cars screamed past them, horns blaring.

Adaq flicked his fingers through the coloured notes. Most were twenties, but there were fifties in there too. Lots of them. The numbers in his head soon couldn't keep up. His breath was short and his mind suddenly fogged up.

Next to him, his sister whooped and slapped the steering wheel.

"This is a good day!" she laughed.

Adaq wanted to laugh too, but nothing came out. Where was his flood of happiness? There must have been a thousand pounds in his hands. Even after he split it with Maya he'd still be the richest 13-year-old he knew. But he couldn't smile. A dead weight was pulling his stomach downwards.

"We can't keep this," he said, finally, forcing the words out between breaths.

"What?" Maya wasn't sure she'd heard him right. "Someone did see you? I knew it!" she said sharply.

"No. Nobody saw me. But..."

Adaq's head throbbed and he wanted to be sick. I can't do this any more, he thought. He shoved the money back into the soft leather wallet.

"What are you doing?" Maya said, grabbing at his hands.

"I'm serious. We should have stopped doing this ages ago." For so long Adaq had wanted to be like Maya – she was the coolest big sister anybody could wish for. But he felt the weight of the wallet in his lap and all he could think was, what sort of person does this?

"I can't believe you!" said Maya. "How ungrateful can you be?"

"It's just wrong! You know it is!"

"All of a sudden? You didn't think it was wrong yesterday, did you? Or when you could buy those trainers?"

Adaq clenched his teeth. His sister had a point. But he'd always told himself there were limits. Like never using the credit cards. And never stealing from anyone who didn't look like they could afford to lose a bit of cash. But for the first time Adaq realised that maybe you only know what your limit is once you've screeched way past it.

"You done talking?" Maya asked calmly. "I want to head back... get one more for the day." She glanced at her watch.

"One more?" Adaq couldn't believe it. "Why do we need one more? Isn't this enough? I'm done! I'm finished."

"Finished? That's not up to you, you..." Maya took a deep breath and tried to laugh again, as if this was just a normal family squabble. "You owe me, OK? I've taught you, I've looked after you. And I've given you half.

Everything's 50–50, even though I pay for it all, including this car. I'm the one taking more of a risk and—"

"You?" spat Adaq, bunching up his fists. "I'm the one who lifts the wallets."

"But I'm way more visible! You think this bit's easy?" She took a stick of chalk from her pocket and waggled it in the air like an exclamation mark.

Lifters have a lot of different techniques, but they work best in pairs. Maya selected the target and worked out which pocket their wallet was in – usually she'd just knock into them and watch which pocket they checked a second later. Once she knew, a simple chalk mark on the target's back gave Adaq all the information he needed to lift the wallet, while Maya drove the car round to the pick-up point.

"But if I got caught I'd…"

"You'd what? You're not old enough to go to prison." Maya was deliberately staying very calm now. It was so frustrating for Adaq he had to fight to stop himself lashing out. "They'd never catch you anyway," she went on. "You're too quick. And who's going to follow you? I don't think the police do a training course in free running, do they?"

"That's not the point!" Adaq yelled at the top of his voice. He snatched up the wallet and shoved open the car door, bursting out onto the pavement. He stormed a few paces into the shadows of the bridge, but after a few strides his fury cleared. He had nowhere to go.

"Sorry," Maya called out through the open car door.

Adaq lowered his shoulders. What would he do without his sister? What sort of a life would he have? At least she'd taught him something while school had beaten his mind and spirit every single day. And she'd looked out for him while everything was going on at home. That would never change.

Gradually, he felt the muscles throughout his body relax. When he lifted his head, he was shocked to see someone in the darkness watching him: a homeless man sitting under the arch of the railway bridge, swamped in a coat and sleeping bag. His eyes just had enough space to peek out below the rim of his cap and above the wild clumps of beard.

Without even thinking, Adaq pulled out a fat handful of cash from the wallet and thrust it at the homeless man.

"Merry Christmas," Adaq muttered, then ran back to the car.

"It's July!" called out the man, but Adaq had already slammed the car door.

"OK. Let's go. One more."

"I knew it," said Maya softly, leaning over to kiss him. "You'll never give up on me." She checked her watch again. Out of the corner of his eye, Adaq saw a strange smile flash across her face. What was she thinking?

He let the moment of doubt die.

Maya moved off into the flow of traffic and muttered, "We're on a roll."

Chapter Two

Special Agent Chris Tenzer kept his eyes level but leaned slightly into his lapel and said, softly, "I'm in the pocket."

An acknowledgement came back in his earpiece straightaway and he moved through the crowd, his eyes locked onto the back of a young businessman's head. It was another warm evening, bustling with workers from the skyscrapers that encased the square. The subject of the surveillance operation blended in perfectly, and right now Agent Tenzer was the only one with a direct view – he was "in the pocket".

They crossed the middle of the square, one man a shadow of the other, only about four metres between them. A rush of people filled the space. Tenzer had to bob his head to catch glimpses of his subject. Suddenly, the businessman lurched to one side. Someone had jostled him – hard.

Tenzer's instincts were sharp and he knew the case thoroughly. Was it one of the subject's contacts in organised crime? Then Agent Tenzer saw a teenage girl hurrying away and he relaxed slightly – this time it looked like just an innocent bump.

Tenzer shifted direction to avoid catching up with his subject, but the sun glared off a high office window right into his eyes. As soon as he could see again, he spotted the white mark on the businessman's shoulder. He knew exactly what that indicated.

"We have a problem," he muttered into his lapel. But he was too late. He didn't spot the lean teenage boy weaving through the crowd until his subject had already been robbed.

"A boy!" said Tenzer into his mic. "I'm sure that boy just picked his pocket. Control, please advise. Something's happening here. I think the package is..."

That was the moment the world

seemed to shatter into pieces. Tenzer's words were drowned out by a massive CRACK. It echoed off every building. Every person in the square flinched, then froze. Dozens of pigeons flapped up from the pavement in an eruption of grey.

But amongst the grey was a spurt of red.

After a second of silence, shrieks split the air. Tenzer's heart rate doubled, but his training took control. His eyes scanned ahead: people scattering, running, screaming... But where was the subject? Waves of people rushing away left a hole in the centre of the crowd, like ripples from a stone dropped in a puddle. And at the centre was a second pool, also growing, but more slowly – blood spreading under a body.

"Subject is down!" Tenzer rushed forwards, into the blood, and crouched. In an instant he knew the man was dead, but again his training kept him calm.

"Sniper," he announced into his lapel. His eyes scanned the buildings around him. The shot could have come from any rooftop, any window. In his earpiece, Control was ordering him to find cover. Tenzer knew he was exposed, but he'd spotted something else.

Among the panic and chaos, one figure was moving more slowly: a teenage boy. Tenzer watched him staggering back, transfixed by the body on the ground. Blood spattered the boy's hoodie and he was clutching something. Even at a distance Tenzer could see the fear in his eyes. Almost in slow motion, the boy moved his stare from the body to Tenzer. They were eye to eye. Sirens and screams blended together. The smell of blood bloomed in the heat.

"He has the package," Tenzer whispered, almost to himself. "He must have it." He forced aside his confusion and looked back at the body. His hands expertly searched every pocket, every potential hiding place. Nothing. When he looked up again the boy was gone.

"Control! Seal the area!" The power was back in Tenzer's voice. "Subject is dead. Pursuing new subject: male, early teens, about 170cm, dark hair, olive complexion, grey hoodie with blood splatter. He has the package."

He's got it, Tenzer thought. He must have.

Special Agent Chris Tenzer thrust his legs into a sprint, but doubt attacked his mind with equal power.

If he's got it, Tenzer thought, does he know what he's got?

Chapter Three

was back in Jenner's voice. Subject

When Adaq heard the sniper's gunshot he thought it was a firework. Only the spots of hot blood exploding onto the side of his face made him turn to look. He watched the businessman crumple. Less than a second before, Adaq's fingers had slipped inside the man's jacket. He'd been close enough to feel his breath and body heat. Now that red heat was oozing out, staining the paving stones.

Adaq wanted to move but couldn't feel his legs. He couldn't even blink.

Then he saw one man rush in the opposite direction from everybody else — towards the body. What was happening? Move, Adaq told himself, but at the same time his brain refused to believe any of this was real. The man looked up at him. The stare felt like a clamp round Adaq's lungs. Still he couldn't unfreeze his limbs.

What snapped Adaq back to life was the sight of the man talking into his lapel. That one small gesture of dropping his chin to speak made every other clue obvious: the physique, the policeman's haircut, the heavy boots on a hot day...

Time to run. Adaq finally broke free. He didn't know how, but his legs were pumping now. The rest of him was still numb. The numbness reached all the way to his fingertips. All the way to the small packet he'd just lifted from a dead man's pocket.

Without looking round, he knew the man in the suit was coming after him. Adaq bolted up a side street, deliberately heading where it was busiest so he would be harder to follow. But it was a mistake. Panic was ripping through the street, electrifying the crowd. People jostled in every direction, so unpredictable that Adaq was constantly blocked.

Enough. He leapt up onto an iron railing. It's conspicuous, he thought, but I have to get to the car. The rail was barely 5cm wide – but Adaq had skills. The balls of his feet were precision springs, powering this human motor. He launched off the rail onto a bollard, like a raindrop hitting a pinhead. His momentum kept him balanced and he skimmed the tops of a dozen bollards until he was free of the crowd.

He dashed across the next road, between snarling cars and trucks. He even used the bonnet of a taxi to bounce himself further ahead of his pursuer. He couldn't glance back. No time. But the reflection in a glass building gave him a glimpse of Tenzer, powering after him, and the blue flashes of police cars in pursuit.

At last – the meeting point. The car engine was running and the passenger door was open. Adaq dived in and the car leapt forward before he'd even hit the seat.

"You got the packet?" Maya asked.

"He was shot," Adaq panted. "The man was shot. That second... it was, like... he's dead..."

"Did you get it?" she demanded.

The car darted onwards, weaving between traffic, mounting the kerb, always moving.

"I saw him... lying there... he's dead... he was shot... I took it and..."

Suddenly, the car lurched round a corner, into a multi-storey car park.

"Where are you going?" asked Adaq.

"It's OK," said Maya, her voice

trembling. She tore up the ramps to the fourth level and expertly reversed into a bay. Adaq wiped his hands across his face, then looked down at them. They were streaked with the dead man's blood. He only realised how much he was shaking when his sister cut the engine and turned to hold his hands steady. Adaq looked into her eyes, searching for reassurance.

"It was so... it was..." He was breathing too hard to get the words out. "He was shot."

"Are you OK?" Maya asked.

"What? Yes. I mean, I think. But..." He trailed off because now his brain had started working. He pulled his hands away.

"Why did you call it a packet?"

Maya didn't respond.

"Before," Adaq insisted. "What did you mean?"

"You know," said Maya. "Packet, wallet, package – whatever."

Adaq punched his hand into his pocket and pulled out what he'd stolen from the dead man: a brown, padded envelope about the same size as a wallet.

"A packet," he said, almost to himself. "You knew..." He stared at his sister. "What's going on?"

Maya's eyes darted to the corner of the car park, then she checked her watch.

"Maya? Why are we here? What is this?"

"How do I know?" Maya snapped.

Adaq tried to order his thoughts, but everything was jumbled. In his head he heard an echo of the crack of the sniper's rifle. It jolted him into action and he tore at the packet in his hands.

"No!" Maya grabbed at the packet, but Adaq held it away from her, right up against the passenger window. They glared at each other. What has she done? Adaq thought, trying to read her face. For the first time in their lives he saw real fear there.

"Don't do this, Adaq," she whispered. "I'm sorry. I should have told you. But..."

"Told me what?"

Maya's eyes were pleading. "Some men offered me forty grand to..." She nodded towards the packet. "Told me the time and place. Showed me a picture. They didn't tell me anyone was going to get..."

"Men? What men?"

"Serious men, Adaq."

"Serious!" Adaq yelled. "Do I look like I'm joking?"

"Some kind of gang." Maya couldn't look at him any more. "Organised crime. They didn't say and I didn't ask."

Suddenly the passenger door was wrenched open and the packet snatched from Adaq's hand.

"Pleasure doing business." The voice was like sweat.

Adaq turned to see an old man in a full-length coat. He slung a briefcase onto Adaq's lap and shuffled away with the packet.

"Dump the car," the old man shouted over his shoulder. "They're closing in."

That's when the blare of sirens flooded up from the street.

"How do we get away?" Maya shouted, jumping out of the car. Adaq followed, his hand closing on the handle of the briefcase. Blue flashes crept closer up the ramp.

"Don't care," the old man called out.

He pointed at Adaq. "He'll be fine. I watched him from the roof. He's like I used to be."

Suddenly, the old man leapt out over a side wall. Adaq was shocked by the athleticism of his movements, then shocked again at the glimpse of a rifle under his coat.

Chapter Four

"Freeze!" Adaq spun round. The agent from the square ran out from between two parked cars, his handgun targeting them. A police car screeched up the ramp behind him. Adaq glanced at Maya, pure terror shredding his senses.

"Wait!" she yelled.

Was she crying? Suddenly, she was running – towards Agent Tenzer. To get away down the ramp? Adaq wondered. Or to draw the police away from him? It gave him the chance he needed.

Instinctively, he sprinted after the sniper and hurdled the wall.

Before he had time to panic, the drop was over. It was only a single storey down to an adjoining rooftop. Adaq found the sniper's crash-mat waiting for him. Adrenaline was making him numb again, and all he could hear were the shouts and sirens from the car park.

One thought pumped through his mind: Maya. Why didn't I look back? I should have looked back for Maya.

When he reached the street he ran – but he only got as far as the next corner. Because there, sitting casually on a bench, was the sniper.

Adaq stared. The old man grinned at

him, cracking his face into folds
of stone.

"You could do my job one day,"
he growled. "If things go that way."

"What?" To Adaq, nothing made
sense any more.

"For now, you'd better run. Nobody's
looking for me. But you..." The sniper
shrugged.

"My sister..." Adaq panted.

"You're better off without her. Get a
future." The sniper gave a nod and only
now did Adaq realise what was still
clamped in his hand – the briefcase.
Suddenly it felt heavy. Adaq's eyes
flicked to the packet on the sniper's lap.

"What is it?" he asked. "What's

worth forty grand?"

The sniper grinned again and pulled out the contents of the packet – a phone.

"Information," he smirked. "And it's worth much more than forty grand."

The sniper shuffled away, pulling the coat around him, even though it was still perfectly warm.

"Catch you later," he said, without turning round. He pressed some buttons and put the phone to his ear as the call connected. The conversation was too faint for Adaq to hear, drowned out by the sirens closing in again.

More than forty grand, Adaq repeated to himself as he glanced back in the direction he had run from. His head pounded, his stomach churned. Forty grand and my sister.

When he looked back at the bench, the sniper's place had been taken by a homeless man.

The briefcase slipped a little in Adaq's hand.

About the author

This story began as an idea for a movie. When it looked like the movie wasn't going to happen, I spent a bit more time on the idea and adapted it so I could write it as a book.

I wrote it over the course of two afternoons in a café in Kings Cross, called Drink, Shop & Do. While writing it I consumed four chocolate brownies and probably a dozen cups of oolong tea.

At the time I was also writing songs for an album, so I named Adaq after the brilliant sound engineer who recorded me singing. It's still his face that I picture when I imagine the character in this book. (By the way, you can hear the songs at www. joecraig.bandcamp.com)

Originally **Lifters** revolved around a pen that contained a biological weapon. But a story about a terrorist threat to a city made it more difficult to focus on the inner lives of the characters, their relationships and what they cared about. The city's going to disintegrate into chaos! Everybody's going to die! Get out of there! That kind of thing. It swamped everything else and got a little silly, so I changed it.

Then for a long time I didn't want to reveal what was in the packet that Adaq stole at all. But I always knew at the back of my mind that wasn't fair to the reader. It's still not really explained in the finished story, because although you discover that it's a phone containing "information", you never find out anything more than that. What sort of information is it and why is it so valuable?

Ultimately, to me, that doesn't matter. **Lifters** is not a story about "information". It's a story about Adaq: what's his place in the world? What's his relationship with his sister? How does he see himself? My aim was that all of those three things would change very quickly, and by the end of the story all three layers of his world would be transformed forever. Now get out of here! Everybody's going to die!

Joe Craig, August 2011

www.joecraig.co.uk

Get in touch with Joe through his website, Facebook (www.facebook.com/jcpages.joecraig) or Twitter (twitter.com/joecraiguk)

Ali Sparkes

freak of
fortune

From the author of Frozen in Time,
winner of the Blue Peter Book of the Year 2010

EDGE

There was a roaring sound in Nic's ears. He guessed he must be really angry – he'd never heard that before. He didn't see Rav jump up from where he'd fallen – slamming headfirst into Nic's stomach. The impact winded Nic and sent him rolling onto the gritty edge of the road, sucking in air like a landed fish. The roaring got louder. The weeping sky darkened a shade past charcoal.

Rav was above him, shaking with rage and the panic of unfamiliar violence. His black hair hung in clumps, showering drips as he nodded jerkily. "Not so good, is it? When someone hits back!"

"Get off!" shouted Nic.

"Coward!" spat Rav.

"NO! Get OFF!" screamed Nic. "We've got to RUN!"

The terror in his enemy's eyes made Rav look back over his shoulder.

He opened his mouth to join in the screaming. A second later it was full of water and his body was spinning over the side of the bridge.

Want to find out if Nic and Rav survive? Get hold of a copy of Freak of Fortune today!

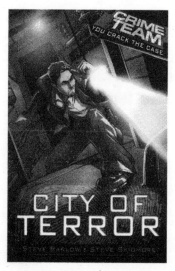